Enid

THE SECRET SEVEN

AN AFTERNOON WITH
THE SECRET SEVEN

Enid Blyton®

THE SECRET SEVEN

AN AFTERNOON WITH THE SECRET SEVEN

Illustrated by Tony Ross

Hodder
Children's
Books

THE SECRET SEVEN

PETER   JANET   JACK   COLIN

GEORGE   PAM   BARBARA

Have you read them all?

... now try the full-length **SECRET SEVEN** mysteries:

SCAMPER

Hodder Children's Books
An imprint of Hachette Children's Group
Part of Hodder & Stoughton
Carmelite House
50 Victoria Embankment
London EC4Y 0DZ
An Hachette UK company

www.hachette.co.uk

CHAPTER ONE

The Secret Seven were having
a meeting.

The shed door was shut
tight. A curtain was drawn
across the little window, in

case Susie, Jack's sister, should make herself a nuisance and come peeping in, as she sometimes did.

The Seven were inside the shed, drinking lemonade given by Peter's mother and eating peppermints brought by Colin.

'This is rather a *dull* meeting,' said Barbara, bored. 'I thought we were going to plan something to do when you called the meeting, Peter – but we haven't planned *anything*.'

'Well, nobody had any good ideas,' said Peter. 'It's not my fault if you're all dozy today.'

'Well, you're as dozy as the rest of us!' said George. 'I suppose it's because it's such a hot summer day – honestly,

I'm melting in this shed.'

'**Wuff**,' said Scamper, the golden spaniel, as if he quite agreed. He lay on the floor, panting.

'He says he's worse off than we are because he has to wear a fur coat, and we're all in short-sleeved shirts or dresses,' said Jack with a grin.

'Listen – someone's coming!' said Janet suddenly. They listened and heard the tip-tap of footsteps coming down the path to the shed.

Then there came a knock at the door.

CHAPTER TWO

'**Password**!' yelled Peter at once.

'Sorry. I don't know it,' said a voice.

'Oh, Mother – I didn't

know it was you,' said Peter. 'Have you come to bring us some more lemonade as you said you would?'

He opened the door, and there stood his mother with a big jug in her hand. She smiled at them all. 'Yes – here's the lemonade – with ice in it this time. My word, you do look hot! Haven't you finished your meeting yet?'

'Well, yes – I suppose
we have,' said Peter. 'But
we haven't settled much, I
must say. We wanted to plan
something exciting to do – but

we can't think of *anything*, Mother!'

'Well, how would you like to help me at the Garden Party in the vicarage garden this afternoon?' asked his mother. 'I could do with some sensible helpers like you.'

'Oh – I'd *like* to help,' said Barbara at once, and Pam nodded too. 'Garden parties are fun.'

'Will there be anything to eat?' asked George.

'I will buy you a nice tea there, and an ice cream each if you'd like to help,' said Peter's mother. 'The five Harris children were coming to help,

but one of them has measles, so none of them can come. You'd do very well instead!'

'We'll come and help for *nothing*,' said Jack. 'My mother's going too – *she*'ll buy me my tea.'

'What do you want us to do?' asked Pam.

'All kinds of things,' said Peter's mother. 'But I'd particularly like you to help with the hoopla stall and the coconut shy next to it. The Harris children were going to run those themselves.'

'Oooh – it sounds fun,' said Colin. 'What time shall we be there, please?'

'At half-past two sharp,' said Peter's mother. 'Washed, brushed and tidy, please. I'll expect you all punctually!' And away she went back to the house.

'Well – we've got something exciting to do, after all!' said Peter, pleased. 'Pour out the lemonade, Janet – I just seem never to stop feeling thirsty in this weather – and let's get out of this hot shed now our meeting is ended.'

CHAPTER THREE

At half-past two all the

members of the Secret Seven

were waiting in the vicarage

garden, just by the hoopla stall,

Scamper as well. A tall lady

came bustling up, smiling.

'Ah – you're the Secret Seven, aren't you?' she said. 'Peter's mother said you would be here. She's busy with the cutting of sandwiches for

tea, and asked me to tell you what to do. Four of you are to manage the hoopla stall – and three the coconut shy. Now – do you know how to run them?'

'Yes, thank you, Mrs James,' said Janet. 'Peter and I have had a hoopla stall before, and a coconut shy is easy.'

'There's just one thing,' said Mrs James. 'You must be

very careful with the money.
You see, sometimes not very
honest people come to garden
sales, and if you should happen
to leave your money bag
unattended for a few minutes,
it might be stolen – and we do
need every penny we can get
this afternoon.'

'We'll be very careful, Mrs
James,' said Peter. He turned
to the others. 'Get busy now.

Janet, Pam, George and I will manage the hoopla stall – and you, Colin, can manage the coconut shy with Barbara and Jack. One to take the money, one to set up the coconuts when they are knocked down, and one to give out the balls to throw at the coconuts.'

'Right,' said Colin, feeling important, and he and Jack began to set up the coconuts in their places. Peter and Janet set out the things meant for the hoopla stall.

George tried the rings over each one to make sure that none was too big to be covered.

Pam began to shout. 'Hoopla! Try your luck! Three rings for sixpence! Win a toy, or a bar of chocolate! Win a butter dish or a little vase – or this pack of cards!'

Chapter Four

People soon came up to the hoopla stall and the coconut shy. The Secret Seven worked very hard indeed, and even Scamper joined in, picking up any hoopla rings that slithered off the stall after being thrown.

It was fun. Great fun! Pam shouted each time people came near, and Janet gave out the wooden rings and took the money. George and Peter watched the rings being thrown, gathered them up and gave them to Janet. When anyone threw a ring that fell completely round one of the things on the stall, Peter gave the article to the customer with a polite little bow.

'**Congratulations**!' he said. 'You have won this beautiful prize!'

The money was put into Peter's cap. He had forgotten to bring a bag of some kind, but his cap did just as well. Janet threw all the money she

took into the cap, and carefully counted out any change necessary.

The three at the coconut shy were doing well. Jack took the money and gave out the balls. He had no cap to put the money into, so he simply slid it into his shorts pocket each time – and that pocket soon began to feel very heavy!

'Only four people have

won a coconut,' he told Peter, when he had a minute to spare. 'That's all! We still have plenty of coconuts left. I say

– shall I put my money into your cap? I'm sure it will make a hole in my pocket soon, I've

taken so much.'

'Yes, put it there,' said Peter. 'Look, you've got another customer. Hurry.'

Presently, about four o'clock, Peter's mother came up, smiling all over her face. 'I hear you Seven are doing very well,' she said. 'You do look hot, standing out here in the sun. What about some tea? And there are lovely

ice creams. Leave one of the
Seven in charge of the stalls
just for now, to see that no
one comes along and makes
off with a coconut or a hoopla
prize. He can have his tea
afterwards.'

'I'll stay,' said Peter. 'I'm
head of the Seven. Go on, you
others – I'll be in charge here.
Scamper, you go, too.'

But Scamper wouldn't

leave Peter. He stayed behind waiting for more hoopla rings to pick up, but as most of the visitors were now having tea and ice creams, there were no customers at all.

Chapter Five

Peter felt bored. He began to rearrange some of the hoopla things when someone called him. 'Hey, Peter! Come and have a ride on my pony!

I've no customers just now, nor have you.'

It was Fred Hilton, who had brought his pony to the Garden Party and was taking quite a lot of money giving sixpenny rides to children.

'Well – I'm really in charge of these two stalls,' said Peter, longing to ride the frisky little pony.

'Leave Scamper on guard,'

said Fred. 'He'd never allow anyone to meddle with the stalls. Anyway, there's nobody about at all. Come on!'

'Right,' said Peter. 'Scamper – you're on guard, see? Look, I'll put my cap of money under the hoopla stall. Nobody must touch it, Scamper – or anything else either. Now, lie down – you're on guard.'

Scamper lay down, looking very important. He kept his eye on the cap of money. Peter went off happily with Fred.

'I'll give you a longer ride than anyone,' said Fred. 'All round this big garden three times!'

By the time Peter had gone round three times, the other members of the Secret Seven had finished their tea and had come back to the stall.

'Where's Peter?' said Barbara. 'Oh, there he is, look – just jumping off Fred's pony.

Peter, Peter – you're to go and
have your tea now – and there
are two ice creams waiting for
you!'

Peter waved his hand and

ran off to the tea tent, calling his thanks to Fred.

My – what a tea! All kinds of sandwiches, piles of little cakes, slices of creamy chocolate cake – and what **enormous** ice creams!

CHAPTER SIX

Peter spent at least twenty
minutes over his tea, and then
went back to the hoopla stall,
feeling much better.

Janet called to him as

soon as he came. 'What did you do with the money, Peter? I wanted some change and I simply *couldn't* find your cap with the money in it.'

'It's under the hoopla stall!' said Peter. 'I hid it there, and left Scamper on guard.'

'Well, it isn't there now,' said Janet, looking suddenly worried. 'I looked everywhere for it. Oh, Peter – and there was such a *lot* of money, too!'

Peter went to look under the stall at the back, where he had put his cap full of money.

Certainly it was not there now. His heart sank. Why, oh why had he gone off to have a ride on Fred's pony! And where was Scamper? He had left him on guard.

'I expect Scamper went off somewhere, too,' said Colin. 'He saw you going off with a friend – and I bet he went off with someone, too – that little Scottie, I expect –

he always loves to frisk about with him.'

'But – but there was *nobody* about, nobody near the stall at all!' said poor Peter, bewildered. 'I looked each time I rode past. I couldn't see Scamper, but I felt sure he was still lying beside my cap, where I had left him. Gosh – this is simply awful. Whatever are we to do?'

'You'd better tell your
mother,' said Pam, looking
rather white. 'Someone's robbed
us – and it was such a lot of
money. We were in charge, too

– oh, why did you go off with Fred?'

Peter went to find his mother, feeling scared and upset. He thought crossly about Scamper. What did he mean by going off when he was on guard? He knew perfectly well what 'on guard' meant – and usually he never, never left the thing he was told to guard. But he must have left the cap of money or it would not have been stolen!

'Your mother's gone home for half an hour,' said Mrs James. 'Just to feed the hens,

I think she said. She'll be back soon.'

Peter wondered what to do. Then he decided to go home and tell his mother before she came back. He would have a chance then to open his money box and take out all the money there, to help to pay back what had been stolen.

CHAPTER SEVEN

He called to Janet as he passed
the hoopla stall. 'I'm going to
slip home for a minute – and
get my money box – and tell
Mother what's happened.

She's gone back to feed the hens. Look after the stalls, all of you – and mind you scold Scamper well when he comes back, Janet.'

He ran all the way home, panting. Just outside the front gate he saw something shining on the path. It was a shilling!

'Well, that's a bit of luck!' said Peter, and picked it up. He opened the gate – and there, on the other side, was a sixpence! He picked that up, too, and went on to the door.

On the mat were two pennies! 'Most mysterious,' thought Peter. 'Perhaps Mother has a hole in her pocket and these dropped out!'

'Mother!' he called, opening the door. 'Mother! Are you here? I want to tell you something.'

Just as his mother called
back to him, Peter heard a
noise. '**Wuff, Wuff, Wuff**!'

It was Scamper's bark.
Had Scamper run off home
then, bored at being alone?

'Is Scamper home,
Mother?' he said, running to
find her.

'Yes – he's in his basket
– and I don't think he can be
very well!' said his mother. 'He
growls every time I go near
him! But why have you come
back – you ought to be in

charge of the hoopla stall!'

'Mother – all the money we took is gone,' said Peter. 'I left Scamper guarding it under the hoopla stall, while I went for a ride on Fred's pony – and

when I got back the cap of money was gone!'

'Oh, *Peter*!' said his mother, shocked. 'How *could* you let such a thing happen!'

'Well, I left Scamper on guard,' said Peter. 'Scamper – where are you? My word, I do feel angry with you – letting me down like that!'

CHAPTER EIGHT

Scamper sat up in his basket.
'Come here,' said Peter sternly.
Scamper put his head down
and rummaged about in his
rug. Then he leapt out of the

basket and ran to Peter – and dropped something at his feet.

It was the capful of money! Scamper looked up at Peter and wagged his tail as if to say, 'Well, I guarded it, you see! I didn't know where you'd gone, so I took it home for you. It's quite safe!'

'Scamper! So *you've* got my cap of money!' said Peter, his heart suddenly much

lighter. 'I suppose the money
I found by the gate and by the
door must have dropped out
when you pushed them open!
Oh, Scamper – did you get

lonely without me? Didn't you know I'd gone for a ride on Fred's pony? Silly dog – you only had to wait a little while!'

'You shouldn't really have gone off on the pony,' said his mother. 'Still – all's well that ends well. Now, hadn't you better go back to your job? See – here is an old bag of mine. Put the money into it – and *guard it yourself.*'

Peter raced back to
the vicarage, feeling most
relieved, Scamper at his heels.
How glad the others were to
see him and hear what had
happened!

'Good old Scamper,' said
Janet, patting him. 'You went
to find Peter, didn't you? And
you took the money with you
because you were guarding it.
You're a very, very good dog.

Come and have an ice cream!'

'Wuff!' said Scamper,

pleased, and off he went with

Janet, leaving the others to sell

the wooden rings and balls to

customers at the hoopla stall
and the coconut shy.

And, as you can guess,
EVERY ONE of the Secret
Seven kept their eyes on the
money after that – and when
all the stalls counted out their
takings, the money brought in
by the Secret Seven was more
than that taken at any other
stall. How very proud they
felt!

'Well done, you Seven,' said Mrs James. 'We really couldn't have done without you!'

'**Wuff**!' said Scamper at once – and, as Janet said, that meant, 'And you CERTAINLY couldn't have done without ME!'

START YOUR
SECRET SEVEN CLUB

each of the Tony Ross editions of The Secret Seven is a Club Token (see below).
Collect any five tokens and you'll get a brilliant Secret Seven club pack –
perfect for you and your friends to start your very own secret club!

GET THE SECRET SEVEN CLUB PACK:

7 club pencils   **7 club bookmarks**   **1 club poster**   **7 club badges**

Simply fill in the form below, send it in with your
five tokens, and we'll send you the club pack!

Send to:

**Secret Seven Club, Hachette Children's Group,
Marketing Department, Carmelite House,
50 Victoria Embankment, London, EC4Y 0DZ**

Closing date: 31st December 2016

TERMS AND CONDITIONS:

Open to UK and Republic of Ireland residents only (2) You must provide the email address of a parent or guardian for your entry to be [vali]d (3) Photocopied tokens are not accepted (4) The form must be completed fully for your entry to be valid (5) Club packs are distributed [on a] first come, first served basis while stocks last (6) No part of the offer is exchangeable for cash or any other offer (7) Please allow 28 days [for] delivery (8) Your details will only be used for the purposes of fulfilling this offer and, if you choose [see tick box below], to send email newsletters about Enid Blyton and other great Hachette Children's books, and will never be shared with any third party.

✂ -

[Pl]ease complete using capital letters (UK Residents Only)

[FI]RST NAME:

[SU]RNAME:

[DA]TE OF BIRTH: DD MM YYYY

[AD]DRESS LINE 1:

[AD]DRESS LINE 2:

[AD]DRESS LINE 3:

[PO]STCODE:

[PA]RENT OR GUARDIAN'S EMAIL ADDRESS:

☐ I'd like to receive a regular Enid Blyton email newsletter and information
[ab]out other great Hachette Children's Group (I can unsubscribe at any time).

I SECRET SEVEN
CLUB TOKEN

✂

www.thesecretseven.co.uk